Whispers
among
Gravestones

Love, Destiny and the Secrets of
the Cemetery

FRANK GARCIA

TABLE OF CONTENTS

INTRODUCTION

I n the quiet town of Hollow, where history lingered in every cobblestone and the wind carried whispers of forgotten tales, two souls found themselves on a path that would forever alter their destinies. This was a place where the past and the present intertwined, where gravestones held secrets and stories, and where the bonds of love were woven in the most unexpected corners.

For Lucas Montgomery, the cemetery was both a haven and a testament to the passage of time. An enigmatic figure, he had dedicated his life to the sacred grounds that held the memories of those who had come before. His quiet dedication was mirrored by the town's curious eyes, as they wondered about the two particular graves he tended with an unspoken reverence.

And then, there was Emma Sinclair—a newcomer to Hollow, seeking solace in the tranquility that the town offered. Drawn to the cemetery's quiet beauty, she had no idea that her footsteps would lead her to a man whose presence carried a weight of mystery and depth that captivated her from the very start.

"Whispers among Gravestones" is a story of connection, transformation, and the boundless power of love. From the gentle rustling of leaves to the unspoken conversations that shape lives, this tale explores the profound moments that forever change the course of our lives. Set against the backdrop of a town steeped in history, this narrative invites you to journey alongside Lucas and Emma as their paths converge, and as they discover that love can be found even in the most unexpected of places.

As you immerse yourself in their story, you will see the blossoming of a relationship that defies time and circumstance. You will feel the warmth of their shared laughter, the weight of their unspoken emotions, and the resonance of their connection. But be prepared, dear reader, for a plot twist that will challenge your understanding of fate, love, and the intricate threads that bind us all.

Turn the pages with an open heart, for within these words lies a tale of love that transcends boundaries, a story that invites us to believe in the extraordinary and to cherish the fleeting moments that shape our lives. Welcome to "Whispers among Gravestones," a journey that will linger in your heart long after the last page is turned.

CHAPTER ONE

Whispers Among Gravestones

As the sun began its descent, casting a warm, golden glow across the cobblestone streets of Hollow, Lucas Montgomery strolled through the town with a sense of tranquility. The fading light painted the facades of the quaint shops in a soft, enchanting hue, creating a picturesque scene that seemed straight out of a storybook. The air was filled with a mix of distant laughter, the rustling of leaves, and the faint jingle of wind chimes as they swayed gently in the breeze.

As he walked, the shopkeepers began to close up their charming boutiques and storefronts, their actions accompanied by friendly nods and waves toward Lucas. The scent of freshly baked bread from the bakery mingled with the aroma of brewed coffee from the café nearby, creating an inviting olfactory tapestry that hung in the air.

"Evening, Lucas," called out Mrs. Patterson, the owner of the flower shop, as she arranged a display of vibrant blooms outside her door.

"Good evening, Mrs. Patterson," Lucas replied with a warm smile. "The flowers are looking especially lovely today."

She chuckled softly, her hands deftly arranging a bouquet. She reached up to brush a loose strand of grey hair from her eyes. "You always have a way with words, Lucas," she said. Then, she narrowed her eyes and looked at Lucas from head to toe. "Heading to the cemetery yet again, I see?"

Lucas bit his lip nervously. Mrs. Patterson, like all of the other residents of Hollow, had grown accustomed to Lucas's presence, but few knew him beyond his diligent work. They looked at him with curious eyes, not understanding why a person would spend so much time in a place filled with death.

With a sigh, Lucas nodded, his gaze briefly glancing towards the cemetery in the distance. "Doing my best, as always."

He looked back at Mrs. Patterson, who was staring at him with the same scrutinizing eyes that he had become used to his entire life. He could imagine what she saw; a young man with scraggly red hair, a nose adorned with freckles, and crooked glasses upon his nose. The years had etched lines on his face and a sense of purpose in his heart. His clothes were usually caked with dried mud, lasting evidence of his time spent near the gravestones. He knew that he was out of place here at Hollow, but he had become used to it. After all, he's lived here his whole life.

Mrs. Patterson reached forward and pulled a bouquet of yellow daisies from her stall. She closed her eyes for a moment, as if to make a decision, and then passed the flowers into Lucas' hands.

"Here you are, boy," she said. "Take these with you today, on me."

Lucas couldn't help but smile. He was happy to know that, even though the townsfolk of Hollow didn't quite accept him as their own, they at least had an understanding.

"Thank you, Mrs. Patterson," Lucas said before continuing on his way.

Leaving behind the bustling town center, Lucas continued his walk towards the outskirts of Hollow. The fading sunlight cast long shadows, creating a serene path that led him past rows of charming houses adorned with flowering vines. As he moved, the remaining shopkeepers bid him farewell, their expressions a mixture of curiosity and warmth.

"Take care now, Lucas," called out Mr. Miller, the old man who ran the antique store. "Don't let those ghosts keep you up at night!"

Lucas chuckled softly. "I'll do my best, Mr. Miller. Have a peaceful evening."

The sweet scent of baked goods lingered in the air as he passed the bakery one last time. Mrs. Turner, the baker, leaned on her doorway, a knowing smile on her lips. "Heading to your sanctuary, Lucas?"

He nodded, appreciating her understanding. "Yes, it's my quiet place."

With a wave, Lucas continued his journey, his footsteps echoing on the cobblestones. The houses grew fewer, and the landscape opened up to reveal the tranquil beauty of the countryside. The distant hills and the winding river seemed to echo the passage of time, adding to the sense of serenity that enveloped the town.

As he approached the cemetery, the sky had shifted to hues of dusky purples and deep blues. The stars began to emerge, one by one, like delicate gems in the vast canvas of the night sky. The soft glow of lanterns lit the path within the cemetery, casting a gentle light on the rows of gravestones.

Lucas paused at the entrance, taking a moment to appreciate the quietude that enveloped this sacred space. The two graves that held a special place in his heart awaited him, bathed in the lantern's warm light. The wind whispered through the trees, and the distant sound of crickets created a soothing symphony. There was an air of mystery around those plots, a silent tale that left the townspeople curious but hesitant to inquire.

Lucas knelt down next to the two graves. He placed Mrs. Patterson's flowers on the ground evenly between both headstones and closed his eyes. He closed his eyes, his fingers idly brushing against one of the soft, yellow petals.

He breathed in, and then out. He always found solace among the gravestones, each one a silent witness to both life and death.

Suddenly, a voice broke the silence that had enveloped him for so long.

"Excuse me," a soft voice called. Lucas turned to find a woman standing at the edge of the plot.

Lucas' heart instantly skipped a beat. The gentle nighttime breeze made her long, blonde hair whip gently around her delicate face. Her small hands clutched at the edges of a yellow dress that was also being taken by the wind. Her bright blue eyes held a mixture of curiosity and respect.

"I don't mean to bother you," the woman said, "but, can I join you?"

Lucas was baffled. He was not used to anyone understanding why he came to the cemetery, let alone asking to sit with him. He furrowed his eyebrows and stared at her.

Why would this gorgeous woman want to be here, with me, in this darkening cemetery?

"Sure," Lucas said tentatively, sliding over to offer the woman more room on the grass.

She sat beside him, that yellow dress spreading out around her legs.

"My name is Emma," she said, offering her hand. "Emma Sinclair."

Lucas took her hand in his and immediately felt a jolt of electricity run through his core. He gasped, his heart rate quickening. He looked up and locked eyes with Emma, wondering if she felt the same passionate charge.

"I'm Lucas," he told her in a shaky voice.

"Beautiful night, isn't it?" she asked casually as she pulled her hand away.

Lucas blinked to compose himself. "Yes, it is," he said. "There's something special about the quietude of this place at night."

Emma nodded and responded, "I've noticed. It's what drew me here in the first place."

Lucas raised an eyebrow, intrigued. "Oh? Have you been visiting the cemetery often?"

She nodded again, a hint of a smile tugging at her lips. "Yes. I'm new to Hollow, but the tranquility of this place has a way of soothing the soul."

Lucas's interest was piqued. "Well, welcome to Hollow, Emma."

Emma's eyes lit up. "I've seen you from a distance, and I've always been curious."

Lucas chuckled softly. "I suppose I stand out," he said, "not many people spend this much time in the cemetery."

Emma's gaze turned introspective. "You know, there's something about cemeteries that captivates me. The stories they hold, the lives they represent, it's like they're a bridge between the past and the present."

"I've always believed that every gravestone tells a story," Lucas responded, nodding in agreement, "and it's important to honor those stories."

Her eyes met his, a spark of understanding passing between them. "I moved to Hollow seeking a fresh start, you know. The stories of the past here, they inspire me to look ahead."

Lucas felt a stronger connection forming, a resonance in their words. "I can understand that. Hollow has a way of embracing those who are open to its embrace."

As they spoke, the night grew quieter around them, and the cemetery seemed to hold its breath, as if aware of the shared moment between these two souls. Their conversation flowed naturally, weaving tales of their own experiences, hopes, and dreams.

"It's strange," Emma mused, her eyes softening. "I feel like I've known you for much longer than this conversation"

Lucas smiled, a warmth filling his heart. "Sometimes, connections are formed quickly, like old friends reuniting."

Emma nodded, her gaze never leaving his. "I believe that. And meeting you, Lucas, it's like finding a kindred spirit."

At that moment, a sense of familiarity enveloped them, as if they were two pieces of a puzzle finally clicking into place. The stars above seemed to shine a little brighter as if reflecting the newfound connection between Lucas and Emma.

As they continued to talk, the breeze carried the whispers of the past, mingling them with the present and future. Lucas and Emma, drawn together by the cemetery's tranquility, found in each other a sense of understanding and companionship they had both been seeking.

CHAPTER TWO

Unlikely Bonds

The sun had begun its descent as Lucas walked his familiar path. He was on the way to the cemetery once again, when Mrs. Patterson's shop caught his eye.

Yesterday's flowers were a really nice touch, Lucas realized. *Maybe I should buy another bouquet today.*

The gentle chime of the bell above the door welcomed him as he entered the shop, the delicate aroma of blossoms filling the air.

Rows of colorful blooms adorned the shop, a vibrant tapestry of nature's beauty. Lucas scanned

the array, his gaze eventually settling on a bouquet of roses. Their deep crimson petals held a
solemn elegance, a tribute he felt was fitting for
the graves he cared for so meticulously.

Mrs. Patterson looked up from her arrange-
ment at the sight of Lucas.

"Back so soon, dear? It's always a pleasure to
see you," she said.

Lucas returned her smile, a quiet gratitude
evident in his eyes. "I'm in need of more flowers for the graves," Lucas announced. "The roses
seem appropriate this time."

She nodded in understanding, her eyes
reflecting the respect she held for his task. "Roses
speak of love and remembrance," she states, "A
fine choice."

As she carefully wrapped the bouquet in crisp
white paper, Lucas observed the skillful precision
of her hands.

"Your flowers always add a touch of beauty to
the cemetery, Mrs. Patterson," Lucas mumbled to
her. "They speak when words cannot."

She handed him the bouquet, her expression softening. "It's my way of contributing, just as you do with your care for the graves. It's a labor of love, isn't it?"

Lucas accepted the bouquet, gentle gratitude in his voice. "Indeed, it is. Thank you, Mrs. Patterson," he said.

As Lucas stepped out of the flower shop, a bouquet of roses in hand, his gaze wandered idly through the bustling town center. The last rays of the sun painted the cobblestone streets with a warm glow. However, his attention was quickly captured by a scene that brought a soft smile to his lips.

There, on a simple wooden stool just outside Mrs. Patterson's flower shop, sat a woman with long, blonde hair. It hung over her face, concealing most of her face as she bent over a sketchpad. The woman's focus was entirely absorbed by the colorful blooms displayed in the shop's window. Her pencil moved with purpose, creating lines that translated her observations onto the page.

Emma Sinclair, Lucas realized. *What is she doing?*

Curious, Lucas took a step toward her. He stood on his tiptoes so that he could see what she was scribbling. He was surprised to see that she was sketching the flowers of Mrs. Patterson's shop.

Lucas watched in quiet admiration as Emma's eyes traced the contours of each petal, her brows furrowing slightly in concentration. The delicate strokes of her pencil captured the essence of the flowers, and he could almost see the life of the blossoms being transferred onto the paper. Her passion and dedication were evident in the way she allowed herself to become absorbed in her art.

With a faint smile, he approached her, the bouquet of roses now a silent companion in his grasp. As he drew closer, he noticed her lips moving ever so slightly, a murmur of thoughts that accompanied her creative process. His voice, soft yet carrying a genuine curiosity, broke the gentle silence.

"Capturing the beauty, I see?" he said.

Startled, Emma looked up from her sketch-pad, her eyes meeting Lucas's. A blush tinted her cheeks, but her gaze held a sense of wonder.

"Oh, yes," Emma said. "The flowers here, they're so exquisite. I couldn't resist trying to capture their essence."

Lucas nodded a warm appreciation in his eyes. "You have a gift for bringing out the beauty in things."

Emma's lips curved into a shy smile. "Thank you. I've been drawn to this flower shop since I arrived. Mrs. Patterson's flowers seem to hold stories of their own."

Lucas's gaze drifted to the bouquet he held, then back to Emma. "Much like the stories told by the gravestones in the cemetery."

There was a shared understanding in their exchange, a recognition of the ways in which both of them sought to preserve and honor the tales that existed around them. It was as if their paths had converged not by chance, but by the thread of fate weaving them together.

Emma closed her sketchpad gently, her gaze returning to the bouquet of roses in Lucas's hand. "Roses, the flowers of sentiment," she said. "What are they for?"

Lucas couldn't help himself. He pulled one rose from the bouquet and handed it to Emma.

"These roses are for the graves that hold stories I hold dear," he said. "But, one is for you now."

Emma accepted the bouquet with a soft smile, her fingers brushing against the velvety petals. "Thank you," she said.

In the days that followed, Lucas and Emma's paths continued to cross. One morning, as the sun painted the sky with soft pastels, Lucas spotted Emma at a park, sitting on a bench and reading a book.

He approached with a warm smile. "Good morning, Emma. Another day to embrace the beauty around us?" he asked.

Emma looked up, her eyes lighting up as she recognized him. "Indeed, Lucas. The stories of this town seem to unfold with every dawn."

Lucas joined her on the bench, a sense of companionship in the air. "Are the pages of your book as captivating as the tales you weave with your sketches?"

Emma chuckled, her book resting on her lap. "Not quite, but they're a different kind of escape."

As the sun continued its ascent, their conversation flowed seamlessly, bridging the gap between their creative passions and shared appreciation for Hollow's charm.

On another occasion, the town organized a community event where residents came together to clean up and beautify the town square. Emma and Lucas ended up on the same team, planting flowers and tidying up the area.

"Preserving the present while honoring the past," Emma observed as she carefully planted a new flower.

Lucas nodded, his hands deep in the soil. "Just as we do with the cemetery and your sketches."

As they worked side by side, their shared efforts mirrored their shared values, creating a sense of unity that extended beyond the task at hand.

In these various encounters, Lucas and Emma continued to bond over their appreciation for the town's beauty, their shared passions, and the unique perspectives they brought to their respective crafts. Each interaction deepened their connection, turning chance meetings into cherished moments that wove their own story within the tapestry of Hollow's history.

A week later, under the velvet embrace of the night sky, Lucas found himself once again in his favorite spot within the cemetery. The lantern's gentle glow cast a warm, golden circle around him, illuminating the weathered gravestones that held the stories of generations past. The air was cool and still, carrying with it the faint scent of blooming flowers and the soft murmur of the wind through the trees.

Sitting on the grass before the two graves that had become his companions over the years, Lucas allowed himself a moment of quiet reflection. His fingers absently traced the edges of another bouquet of roses he had brought, each petal a testament to the emotions he felt for those who rested here.

As he gazed out into the serene landscape, his thoughts drifted to Emma. The encounters they'd shared in the town seemed to dance before his mind's eye, the moments of connection, the conversations that flowed effortlessly, and the sense of understanding that seemed to grow with each meeting.

Closing his eyes for a moment, Lucas allowed himself to relive those moments, savoring the genuine connection they had formed. He recalled the way Emma's eyes sparkled with curiosity and how her smile held a warmth that felt like a gentle embrace.

Opening his eyes, he looked down at the roses cradled in his hands, their petals catching the lantern's light. They seemed to symbolize more than just remembrance; they held the potential for new beginnings, much like the fresh start Emma had sought when she arrived in Hollow.

A soft breeze rustled the leaves, and Lucas leaned back, his heart full with a mixture of gratitude and hope. In this quiet corner of the world, under the watchful eyes of the stars, he felt the presence of the stories he tended to and the possibility of a new chapter intertwining with his own.

Suddenly, a faint sound of footsteps reached his ears. He turned his head slightly, surprised by the presence of someone else at this quiet hour.

"Oh, hello, Emma," Lucas said when he saw a glimpse of that blonde hair shining in the starlight. The moonlight painted a silvery path ahead of her, lending an ethereal glow to her figure.

Lucas's eyes met Emma's as she drew closer, her expression one of quiet determination. She stopped a few steps away from his spot on the grass, her presence a gentle interruption to his thoughts.

"May I join you?" she asked, her voice soft and warm in the stillness.

A faint smile tugged at Lucas's lips as he sensed the unspoken invitation. "Of course,

Emma," he replied, his voice carrying a touch of genuine welcome.

With a graceful movement, Emma lowered herself onto the bench beside him. The night seemed to settle around them, their silhouettes etched against the backdrop of the cemetery's beauty. The air held a sense of camaraderie, a connection formed by shared moments and unspoken understandings.

As they sat side by side, a comfortable silence wrapped around them like a familiar embrace. The moonlight bathed the gravestones in a soft glow, and the stars above seemed to shimmer with an added radiance. The stories of the past seemed to weave around them, holding them in their embrace.

Finally, Emma broke the silence, her voice a gentle thread in the quiet tapestry of the night.

"It's a beautiful night, isn't it?" she said,

Lucas turned to her, his eyes reflecting the moon's silver sheen. "Yes, it is. The stories of this place seem to awaken under the moonlight."

Emma nodded, her gaze moving from the gravestones to the roses in Lucas's hand. "The roses are a lovely touch. A tribute to the lives that were," she said.

Lucas glanced at the bouquet, then back at Emma, his eyes conveying a shared sentiment. "Yes, a way to honor the past and the memories it holds," he said. "Speaking of pasts, Emma, if you don't mind me asking, how did you find your way to Hollow? It seems like you have a deep appreciation for this place."

Emma's lips curved into a reflective smile, her eyes momentarily distant. "It's a story of wanderlust and unexpected turns, really."

Intrigued, Lucas leaned in slightly. "I'm all ears."

Taking a thoughtful sip of her coffee, Emma began, "I grew up in a home where my parents had big plans for me. They wanted me to pursue a medical degree, a path they believed was secure and respectable."

Lucas nodded, his expression understanding. "That must have been a significant decision to make."

Emma's eyes held a mixture of emotions as she continued, "I went along with it for a while, but as the years went by, I realized that medicine wasn't where my heart truly belonged. The idea of spending my life in a hospital felt suffocating."

Lucas's empathy was palpable. "Sometimes, the paths others set for us aren't always the ones that align with who we are."

Emma's gaze met his, gratitude shining in her eyes. "Exactly. So, one day, I packed my bags and took off driving. I didn't know where I was headed; I just wanted to escape the expectations of others and discover what truly resonated with me."

Lucas leaned back, a gentle smile curving his lips. "It sounds like quite the journey."

Emma's expression softened. "It was. I traveled from town to town, following the roads without a set destination. And that's how I stumbled upon Hollow."

Lucas's curiosity deepened. "What made you stop here?"

Emma's eyes lit up with a spark of fondness. "It was the cemetery, actually. I happened to drive past it, and something about the tranquility and the history captivated me. I decided to stop and take a walk, and as I wandered among the gravestones, I felt a connection to the stories they held. It was like the weight of my uncertain journey lifted for a moment."

Lucas's gaze held a quiet understanding. "It's a place that has that effect on people."

A soft laugh escaped Emma's lips. "I remember the first time I came here. The calmness of the surroundings allowed me to reflect on where I was, where I wanted to be, and what truly mattered."

Lucas's voice was gentle as he asked, "And what did you find?"

Emma's smile held a touch of wonder. "I found that my heart was drawn to creating, to capturing the beauty around me in sketches. I found that I could make my own path, guided by what brought me joy."

"That is incredible," Lucas said. "Always follow your dreams."

With a gentle smile, Emma turned to him. "Now you know my story," she said. "It's time that I got to know yours. I've noticed you spend a lot of time tending to these two graves. Is there a special reason?"

Lucas's gaze briefly shifted to the gravestones in question, his expression a mixture of fondness and something more profound. He hesitated for a moment before responding, his voice soft. "Yes, there is a reason. They hold a certain significance to me," he responded.

Intrigued by his response, Emma pressed gently, her tone encouraging. "Well, who were they?" she asked.

Lucas's eyes held a distant look as if lost in his thoughts. "Just... two important people."

Emma sensed there was more beneath the surface, a connection that ran deeper than words could convey.

"It seems like there's a personal connection too," she ventured, her gaze thoughtful.

Lucas's lips curved into a slight smile, though his eyes remained guarded. "Perhaps. Some connections go beyond words, beyond what we can comprehend," he states. "Don't you think?"

CHAPTER THREE

Echoes of Affection

Time flowed by like a gentle stream, each day carrying with it the ebb and flow of life in the town of Hollow. As the days turned into weeks, the bond between Lucas and Emma continued to deepen, growing stronger with each shared moment. The cemetery, once a place of solitude, had transformed into a sanctuary where their connection blossomed. Amidst the whispers of the past, they found a haven in each other's presence.

In the midst of this passage of time, Lucas found himself at Mrs. Patterson's shop once again. He had gotten into the habit of buying flowers for the graves. But, this time, his gaze was drawn to a second bouquet.

The thought of Emma had been on his mind, her presence a constant thread weaving through his days. He wanted to convey his feelings, to show her the depth of his regard. And so, he had decided to let the flowers speak for him.

"I'll take that one, too," Lucas told Mrs. Patterson.

Her eyes widened with surprise. She had become used to Lucas buying one bouquet at a time. This was an unexpected change, but she handed the flowers over to him regardless.

With the bouquet cradled gently in his arms, he made his way to the cemetery. The sun painted the sky with hues of gold and orange, casting a warm embrace over the landscape. As he approached their usual meeting spot, he couldn't help but feel a flutter of anticipation mingled with vulnerability.

He spotted Emma sitting on the grass, sketching her heart away. A soft smile played on his lips as he neared her.

"Hello, Emma," he greeted, his voice carrying a touch of warmth.

Emma looked up, her eyes lighting up at his presence. "Lucas, hey!"

He extended the bouquet towards her, his eyes meeting hers with a sincerity that needed no words.

"I brought these for you. Just a small gesture to let you know how much I appreciate your presence in my life," he confessed.

Emma's expression shifted from surprise to a mix of gratitude and a touch of bashfulness. She accepted the bouquet with a genuine smile, her fingers brushing against the petals.

"Thank you, Lucas. They're beautiful," she gushed.

As they shared a moment in the park, the breeze carrying the gentle scent of the flowers, there was a subtle shift in the air. The weeks that had passed had deepened their connection, and this simple yet meaningful gesture was a testament to the emotions that had taken root between them.

With the bouquet nestled in her hands, Emma felt a warmth spreading within her, a realization that sometimes the most meaningful expressions of care came in the form of thoughtful actions. And as they continued their conversation, the extra bouquet of flowers became a symbol of the unspoken feelings that had grown in the heart of the quiet caretaker who had captured her attention from the very beginning.

Not to be outdone, Emma found herself carefully placing a handcrafted bookmark on top of Lucas's gardening tools one morning. The bookmark was a labor of love, adorned with a delicate pressed flower that she had carefully chosen. It was her way of expressing gratitude for the stories he had shared and the moments they had spent together.

A few days later, as they crossed paths in the garden, Lucas held the bookmark in his hand.

"Emma, I found this on my tools," he said, his voice tinged with curiosity.

Emma's cheeks tinged with a soft blush as she met his gaze. "I wanted to show my appreciation for all the stories you've shared with me. The bookmark has a pressed flower from Mrs. Patterson's shop."

Lucas's eyes lit up as he examined the bookmark, his fingers tracing the delicate petals. "Thank you, Emma. This means a lot," he said.

With a quiet smile, she nodded. "It's a token of our growing friendship," she said.

Lucas's expression held a mixture of gratitude and understanding. "I treasure that," he said.

Their words were simple, yet they carried a weight that transcended their casual conversations. As Lucas accepted the bookmark, it was not just a physical token but a bridge between them, a recognition of the connection that had been blossoming between the quiet caretaker and the woman who had brought a new kind of vitality to his world.

Their interactions became filled with these quiet gestures, the unspoken language of affection that only they understood. Lucas would leave a warm cup of coffee for Emma on a particularly chilly morning, and Emma would leave a note of encouragement tucked under the corner of Lucas's gardening journal.

As the autumn leaves gave way to winter's icy embrace, the connection between Lucas and Emma continued to flourish, weathering the changing seasons. The town of Hollow transformed into a winter wonderland, its streets adorned with a blanket of pristine snow.

One day, as snowflakes gently fell from the sky, Lucas and Emma found themselves in the heart of this snowy landscape. Laughter echoed around them as they engaged in a spirited snowball fight, their breath visible in the crisp air. The once-quiet cemetery had become a playground, a canvas of white inviting them to let go of their adult concerns and embrace the childlike joy of the moment.

A snowball soared through the air, narrowly missing Lucas's shoulder. He turned to Emma with a mischievous grin. "You're quite the competitor, Emma!" he called out.

Emma giggled, her cheeks rosy from both the cold and the excitement. "You're not so bad yourself, Lucas!"

They continued to exchange snowballs, each throw accompanied by laughter and the sound of soft impacts. With each snowball that connected or missed its target, the camaraderie between them grew stronger, a shared sense of lightheartedness knitting their souls closer.

Lucas ducked behind a snow-covered bench, gathering snow in his gloved hands. "You won't get away that easily!" he called out playfully.

Emma's laughter rang through the air as she formed a snowball of her own. "We'll see about that!" she giggled.

Snowballs flew back and forth, a dance of friendship amidst the falling snow. As they paused for a moment to catch their breath, their eyes met, sparkling with mirth and connection. The cemetery's solemnity had given way to a shared moment of unadulterated joy, the purity of the snowflakes around them reflecting the simplicity of their laughter.

With a final exchange of snowballs, they both stood breathless but full of life. As the snow settled around them, Lucas and Emma found themselves wrapped in the warmth of each other's company. Their playful snowball fight had become more than just a game; it had become a memory etched into the fabric of their growing bond.

One evening, as Lucas and Emma strolled through the town square, their fingers brushing against each other's in a gesture that had become familiar, they couldn't help but notice the shared glances directed their way. The townspeople's looks held a mix of affection and approval, a silent acknowledgment of the bond that had formed between the quiet caretaker and the woman who had brought new vibrancy to the town.

Emma's gaze met Lucas's, and she couldn't help but chuckle softly.

"I think we might be the latest gossip in town," she remarked, her voice carrying a hint of amusement.

Lucas smiled, a twinkle in his eyes. "It seems that our growing fondness for each other hasn't gone unnoticed," he agreed.

As they walked, the shopkeepers they passed greeted them with knowing smiles and warm nods. It was as if the town itself had become a silent witness to their blossoming relationship, embracing the idea that sometimes, unexpected connections could bring about the most beautiful changes.

A few days later, as they enjoyed a quiet moment by the cemetery's entrance, Emma turned to Lucas with a smile. "It's interesting how our friendship has become a source of interest for everyone," she pointed out.

Lucas nodded, his expression thoughtful. "It's a reminder that sometimes, the most unexpected connections can be the ones that touch people's hearts," he said.

Their gazes met, and in that shared understanding, they acknowledged that their relationship was not just a matter of personal sentiment. It was a testament to the beauty of new beginnings, to the hope that even in the midst of life's complexities, two souls could find solace and companionship in each other's presence.

Then, Emma smiled.

"Hey, I have a surprise for you," she said, a hint of excitement dancing in her eyes as she led Lucas by the hand. His curiosity piqued, he followed her through the town's charming streets until they reached a quaint alleyway nestled between buildings.

As they turned the corner, Lucas's eyes widened in amazement. Before him stretched a beautiful mural, a vibrant depiction of him and Emma sitting side by side near a row of gravestones. The attention to detail was striking, the way their hands intertwined, the gentle smiles on their faces, and the play of light on the gravestones. It was a moment captured in time, painted with love and care.

Emma's gaze never left Lucas as she watched his reaction.

"I thought this mural could be a way to immortalize the moments we've shared, the bond we've built. Just like the memories we've created here," she explained, her voice soft with emotion.

Lucas was speechless, his heart overflowing with a mixture of awe and gratitude. He turned to Emma, his eyes reflecting the depth of his feelings.

"Emma, this is... incredible. You've captured us, our connection, and this place so beautifully."

Emma's cheeks tinged with a hint of blush, and she looked down briefly before meeting his gaze with a warm smile. "I'm glad you like it. This alleyway was like a blank canvas, and I wanted to paint a piece of our story on it."

As they stood before the mural, the scene seemed to encapsulate their journey, their meetings near the gravestones, their shared moments of laughter and understanding. The mural was a testament to the bond they had formed, a reminder of the love and connection that had grown between them.

Lucas reached for Emma's hand, his fingers intertwining with hers. "This mural is not just a surprise, Emma. It's a beautiful representation of the chapters we've written together and the ones we have yet to fill with our love."

As they stood there, hand in hand, before the mural that captured their unique story, a sense of hope and anticipation filled the air. The mural would forever stand as a symbol of their journey, a visual reminder of the love they had nurtured in the heart of Hollow.

CHAPTER FOUR

Hearts Unveiled

With the approach of the annual Winter Festival, Hollow transformed into a lively scene of activity and excitement. The town bustled with preparations, and the air was filled with a tangible sense of anticipation. As snowflakes fell gently from the sky, Lucas and Emma found themselves becoming swept up in the festive atmosphere.

One afternoon, as they strolled through the town square, their breath visible in the cold air,

Emma's eyes sparkled with delight as she took in the colorful decorations.

"It's amazing how the town comes alive during the Winter Festival," she exclaimed, her voice full of wonder.

Lucas nodded in agreement, a small smile playing on his lips. "It's a time when the spirit of the town truly shines."

As they continued to walk, they noticed children giggling as they decorated the snowmen, and vendors setting up their stalls with holiday treats. The scene was a tapestry of lights, colors, and joyful laughter. In the midst of this festive ambiance, their own bond seemed to mirror the town's excitement. Their steps were lighter, their conversations more animated, and the unspoken emotions between them more vibrant.

Days turned into nights, and soon the festival was in full swing. The town square came alive with twinkling lights, and the aroma of hot cocoa and holiday treats filled the air. Emma and Lucas found themselves attending the festival together, their fingers brushing against each other's as they moved through the crowd.

Under the enchanting glow of fairy lights, Lucas' voice carried a touch of nostalgia. "I used to love coming to this festival as a child. It feels like I've come full circle," he said.

Emma's gaze held a warmth that reached his eyes. "Well, I guess that it's a reminder that even as time moves forward, some traditions and feelings remain constant."

As they stood amidst the festive merriment, the music and laughter swirling around them, their connection seemed to deepen. The twinkling lights above cast a soft glow, reflecting in their eyes. In that moment, amidst the holiday cheer, they felt a surge of emotions they had long kept at bay.

"Hey, do you want to go ice skating?" Emma suggested, glancing at the nearby rink. The ice was sparkling like a mirror in the snow.

"Sure," Lucas agreed.

Before they knew it, their laughter mingled with the crisp winter air as they laced up their skates, fingers brushing occasionally as they helped each other fasten the laces.

Emma steadied herself on the ice, her excitement tinged with a touch of nervousness. "I haven't ice skated in years. I hope I remember how!" she admits.

Lucas chuckled softly, his eyes warm as he held out his hand. "Don't worry, Emma. I'll be right here to catch you if you stumble," he said.

With a smile, she took his hand, her grip firm but her heart racing. They stepped onto the ice, their first few glides were tentative. As they found their rhythm, their movements became more confident, and soon they were skating side by side, laughter echoing around them.

But then, as they attempted a turn, their feet lost traction, and they began to slide. A look of surprise crossed Emma's face, and her arms flailed slightly as she tried to regain her balance. In an instant, Lucas reacted, reaching out and catching her by the waist, his strong arms drawing her closer.

Their laughter turned into a shared moment of surprise, and for a brief second, time seemed to stand still. Emma's heart raced not just from the skating mishap, but from the closeness she felt to Lucas, his touch sending a warm shiver through her.

As they steadied themselves, their gazes locked, the icy ground beneath them melting away as if they were the only two people on the rink. Their breaths intertwined in the frosty air, the world around them fading into the background.

"Are you alright?" Lucas's voice was a gentle whisper, his eyes searching hers with a tenderness that spoke volumes.

Emma's heart skipped a beat, her own voice a hushed reply. "Yeah, I'm fine. Thanks to you."

As they stood, their bodies still intertwined, a blush colored Emma's cheeks, her gaze dropping slightly. Lucas's hand lingered on her waist for a heartbeat longer, his touch sending a ripple of warmth through her.

As they stood on the ice rink, the soft glow of fairy lights illuminating their path, a sense of intimacy surrounded Lucas and Emma. The festive atmosphere seemed to fade into the background, leaving only the two of them in their own world.

Lucas's gaze held a quiet sincerity, his eyes reflecting the depth of his emotions. With a calm but determined voice, he spoke words that had been welling up within him. "Emma, I want you to know that your presence in my life... It's like a spark that's reignited a light I thought had been extinguished long ago."

Emma's heart quickened at his confession, her eyes locking onto his with an intensity that mirrored his sentiment. Her own voice was soft, laced with a vulnerability she hadn't expected to reveal on this icy stage. "Lucas, I feel the same way. Your kindness and the way you've welcomed me into Hollow have brought a warmth to my life that I didn't know I was missing."

Their words hung in the air, suspended in the timeless moment as they continued to skate, their movements guided by the unspoken connection between them. The chill of the winter air seemed to contrast with the warmth that emanated from their heartfelt exchange.

Lucas's gaze never wavered, his eyes tracing the contours of Emma's face as if memorizing every detail. "Emma, I've found myself looking forward to our conversations, to our shared moments. You've become a beacon of light in my everyday routine."

Emma's fingers brushed against his, a gentle touch that conveyed the depth of her feelings. "And you, Lucas, have become an anchor for me in this new chapter of my life. Your stories, your presence, they've made Hollow feel like home."

Lucas was touched by her words. He gently brushed a strand of hair behind her ear. He let his hand linger there as the tension intensified.

"Emma," he whispered, "you are incredible."

He pressed his lips to hers, and at that moment, the world stopped. It was a kiss filled with the promise of a future yet to be written, a future woven with shared dreams and whispered affections. The world seemed to fall away as they embraced, the gentle pressure of their lips a testament to the emotions that had blossomed between them.

As they parted, their eyes met once again, the unspoken words in their gazes carrying a depth of meaning that transcended mere conversation. The festival's enchantment mirrored the enchantment they felt for each other, their connection solidifying in the exchange of that simple, yet profound, kiss.

With their hearts unveiled and their feelings acknowledged, Lucas and Emma embraced the journey that lay ahead. As winter melted into spring, their love story continued to unfold, one chapter at a time, woven into the fabric of Hollow's history and etched among the gravestones that had seen the beginning of their extraordinary journey.

CHAPTER FIVE

Embrace of Commitment

T he town of Hollow had seen the gradual evolution of Lucas and Emma's relationship, from the first whispers of connection to the blossoming of a love that defied the odds. As spring unfurled its vibrant colors, so did their relationship, and the decision to commit to one another became inevitable.

One day, under the gentle warmth of the sun, Lucas carefully arranged a cozy picnic blanket in front of the two gravestones that had become a significant part of his life. The cemetery had transformed from a place of solemnity to a space filled with memories, stories, and now, the promise of shared moments.

Emma watched with a soft smile as Lucas set up the picnic. The air carried the scent of freshly bloomed flowers and the cheerful whispers of nature.

"This is such a beautiful idea, Lucas," she remarked, her voice carrying a touch of admiration.

Lucas's gaze met hers, his own smile filled with a mixture of anticipation and contentment. "I thought it would be a nice way to honor their memory and create new memories together," he told her.

As they settled onto the blanket, the spread before them was a tantalizing feast for the senses. There was a medley of sandwiches, salads, and fruits, each dish prepared with care and creativity. Lucas had also brought a thermos of warm soup and a basket of freshly baked pastries.

Emma's eyes lit up as she took in the array of food. "You've really outdone yourself, Lucas. This all looks amazing."

Lucas's cheeks tinged with a hint of bashfulness. "I wanted to make sure it was a special meal for us."

Emma savored a bite of the sandwich, her eyes meeting Lucas's with a twinkle. "You know, I never thought I'd have a picnic in a cemetery, but this feels so right."

Lucas chuckled, his eyes dancing with amusement. "It's a reminder that even in places of quiet reflection, life and connection can thrive."

They continued to enjoy the food, savoring the flavors and each other's company. The past and the present seemed to intertwine as they wove new memories against the backdrop of the gravestones that had witnessed so much history.

As they indulged in the pastries, their laughter resonated in the air, a melody of happiness that seemed to echo through the cemetery. The sunlight filtered through the leaves, casting dappled patterns on the ground, and the world felt suspended in a bubble of timelessness.

As the sun began to set, casting a warm, golden hue over the cemetery, Lucas took a deep breath, his heart pounding with a blend of vulner-ability and determination. He shifted slightly on the picnic blanket, his fingers nervously grazing the small box he had concealed.

Emma looked at him, her eyes curious and filled with affection. "Is everything okay, Lucas?"

Lucas met her gaze, his own eyes reflecting a mixture of emotions. With a steadiness that came from the depths of his heart, he reached into his pocket and pulled out the small box. Holding it delicately in his hand, he looked into Emma's eyes and spoke with a voice that carried his feelings.

"Emma, you've become such an integral part of my life. The moments we've shared, the connec-tion we've built, it's something I cherish deeply," Lucas' voice broke as he spoke the words.

Emma's breath caught as she saw the box, her heart racing with a sudden realization. Her eyes met Lucas's, and she felt the weight of his words in the air between them.

With a gentle smile, Lucas continued his words resonating with sincerity. "I've realized that I want more than just shared moments and whispered conversations. I want a deeper commitment, a journey where we can face life's challenges and celebrate its joys side by side," he said.

Emma's heart brimmed with emotion as his words sank in. She felt a surge of warmth and happiness, a realization that what they had was truly special.

Lucas's voice held unwavering determination as he opened the box to reveal a delicate ring. "Emma, will you marry me?" he asked.

Emma's face fell. For a moment, it looked like she had been hit by a truck, the shock of Lucas's question was so great.

"Lucas... No," she said.

Without another word, she walked away, leaving Lucas confused and heartbroken.

CHAPTER SIX

Uncertainties

With her heart heavy and her mind in turmoil, Emma found herself drawn to the town square, seeking solace in the act of creation. She set up an easel near the gently splashing fountain, the bubbling water providing a soothing backdrop to the chaos within her. The canvas stood before her, a blank slate waiting to absorb her emotions.

As she dipped her paintbrush into the array of colors, her thoughts swirled like a tempest. She mixed shades that mirrored her uncertainty, the blues reflecting her conflicted emotions and the dark hues encapsulating her fears. With each stroke, the brush carried away a fraction of her pain, replacing it with the tangible expression of her inner turmoil.

Amid the sounds of the town around her, Emma painted with an intensity that bordered on desperation. She let the colors blend and bleed, a visual representation of her heartache and the decisions that weighed on her soul. The strokes were bold and raw, a release of emotions that had been trapped within her.

The scene on the canvas began to take shape, a whirlwind of colors and lines that seemed to mirror the storm raging inside her. She painted without inhibition, allowing her emotions to guide her hand, each stroke a cathartic release. The town's people walked by, some offering curious glances, but Emma was lost in her world of colors and feelings.

As the sun dipped below the horizon, casting a warm golden glow over the square, Emma stepped back to admire her work. The canvas was a reflection of her heart in its rawest form.

Uncertain, torn, and yet somehow beautiful in its honesty.

She had poured her feelings onto the canvas, allowing the paint to become her voice when words failed her.

She closed her eyes, trying to stem the tide of tears that threatened to overwhelm her. Her thoughts were a whirlwind of conflicting emotions, and amidst the chaos, one truth stood out starkly: she had said no to Lucas's proposal.

As the reality of her decision settled in, her heart ached with a mixture of regret and fear. She thought about how she had pursued a medical degree under pressure from her parents, only to realize it wasn't her true calling. The weight of that long commitment had left scars she wasn't ready to forget.

Tears slipped through her fingers as she whispered to herself, her voice quivering with self-doubt.

I can't make another mistake like that, she thought, *another commitment that I might regret.*

As she stared at her painting, she remembered Lucas's sincere proposal, the way his eyes held so much hope and love. She thought about the warmth of his touch, the shared laughter, and the countless moments that had deepened their connection. But her fear of repeating past mistakes had clouded her ability to embrace the future.

Slowly, Emma began to pack up her art supplies. As she did, her heart was heavy with conflicted emotions, the water's soothing sound seemed to echo her turmoil. The town square, usually a place of joy and community, now mirrored the ache within her.

She stood up, wiped her tears away, her gaze drifting towards Mrs. Patterson's flower shop. The memory of Lucas's thoughtfulness and kindness came rushing back. She recalled the many times he had bought flowers, not just for the graves but also to brighten their moments together. The gesture spoke volumes about his heart and his ability to cherish and care.

As she stared at the flower shop's colorful display, a realization began to dawn upon her. Despite her fear of making another mistake, a glimmer of clarity pierced through her turmoil. She knew that no one could predict the future with certainty, but the happiness she felt whenever she was with Lucas couldn't be ignored.

She thought about his warm smile, the way his eyes sparkled when they talked, and the shared laughter that had become a part of their connection. The bond they had wasn't a guarantee against challenges, but it was a testament to their ability to face those challenges together.

With a determined breath, Emma pushed herself up from the fountain's edge. The decision to apologize and seek out Lucas was now crystal clear in her mind. She understood that true happiness sometimes required taking risks, and perhaps that was the lesson she needed to learn from her past mistakes. Her steps were purposeful as she walked towards the heart of town, her heart no longer heavy with doubt but filled with newfound resolution.

Emma made her way to the familiar spot in the cemetery where Lucas sat. The golden sun cast a warm glow over the gravestones, and the air was filled with a sense of anticipation that matched her own emotions.

There he was, Lucas, tending to the grounds with his usual devotion. As she approached, she cleared her throat, her voice carrying a mix of nervousness and sincerity. "Lucas?"

He turned, his eyes lighting up as they met hers. "Emma," he said softly, his gaze a mixture of surprise and welcome.

Taking a deep breath, Emma stepped closer, her heart racing with a blend of anxiety and hope.

"I owe you an apology," she began, her voice sincere. "I'm sorry for my reaction earlier. I've been letting my past fears cloud my judgment."

Lucas's expression softened, his understanding evident. "Emma, it's okay. I understand."

She looked into his eyes, her gaze steady as she continued, her voice gaining strength. "But I want you to know that I've thought a lot about us, about what you mean to me, and about the possibility of a future together."

He listened, his attention unwavering as he gave her the space to express herself.

With a deep breath, Emma confessed her fears, her voice carrying a mixture of vulnerability and determination. "I've made mistakes in the past, decisions that led me down paths I wasn't meant to be on. And I've been so afraid of making another mistake that I let that fear guide my decisions."

She paused, her eyes never leaving his. "But when I look at you, Lucas, and when I think about the moments we've shared, I can't ignore the happiness you bring to my life. I've realized that even though I can't know for certain that it won't be a mistake, marrying you would bring me true happiness."

Her voice trembled slightly as she continued, her heart laid bare before him. "I love you, Lucas. I love you for your kindness, for your strength, and for the way you've shown me that love is worth taking a chance on."

A tender smile formed on Lucas's lips, his eyes shimmering with emotion. "Emma..."

Her gaze held his, her voice unwavering as she spoke the words she had come to say. "So, with all my heart, I would love to marry you."

The world seemed to hold its breath as their eyes locked, their emotions swirling in the space between them. In that moment, beneath the golden sun and amidst the gravestones, the weight of their pasts and the uncertainty of the future fell away, leaving only the profound connection they had forged.

Lucas stepped closer, his hand reaching for hers, their fingers intertwining as they stood together in the embrace of their shared decision. His smile was radiant, his voice filled with love and promise. "Emma, you've just made me the happiest man in the world."

CHAPTER SEVEN

Love Blossoms in Hollow

The weeks leading up to their wedding were a whirlwind of preparations and shared anticipation. The town of Hollow embraced their love story, rallying around Lucas and Emma with unwavering support. The once-silent gravestones had become witnesses to a new beginning, a love story that had sprung from their midst.

Under the brilliant summer sun, its golden rays illuminating the vibrant tapestry of wildflowers that surrounded them, Lucas and Emma stood hand in hand, facing their friends and the townspeople who had become an integral part of their lives. The warm breeze played with Emma's hair, and her heart danced with a mixture of excitement and contentment.

The townspeople had gathered, creating a natural amphitheater among the trees and flowers, their smiling faces a testament to the joy that enveloped the scene. As the murmurs of anticipation settled into hushed anticipation, Lucas and Emma exchanged a glance that held a universe of shared understanding.

The town's beloved minister, known for his wisdom and kindness, began to speak, his words carrying the weight of the occasion. "We are gathered here today to celebrate not only the union of two individuals," he said, "but the merging of two hearts, two lives, and two paths that have found their way to one another."

Lucas's eyes were fixed on Emma, his grip on her hand reassuring and full of promise. He looked into her eyes, his voice steady as he spoke his vows. "Emma, from the moment you entered my life, you brought light, laughter, and a depth of understanding that I never thought I'd find. I promise to cherish every moment we share, to stand by your side in times of joy and adversity, and to love you with a steadfastness that knows no bounds."

Emma's voice was clear and filled with emotion as she recited her vows. "Lucas, you've shown me that love is not just a word, but a choice and a commitment. With you, I've found a partner who supports my dreams and shares in my passions. I promise to stand by you, to encourage you, and to love you through all the seasons of life."

Their words were more than promises; they were declarations of the bond they had forged, a bond that had weathered doubts and fears to emerge stronger and more profound.

As the minister asked for the rings, Lucas and Emma exchanged simple yet elegant bands, each one symbolizing the unending circle of their commitment. Their hands trembled slightly as they slid the rings onto each other's fingers, a physical representation of the unbreakable connection they shared.

And then, with a sense of anticipation that hung in the air like a whispered secret, the moment arrived. With their hands entwined and their hearts beating as one, Lucas and Emma leaned in, their lips meeting in a kiss that spoke of a journey taken and a future embraced. The cheers from the townspeople echoed through the clearing, their happiness adding to the symphony of the moment.

As they pulled away, their eyes met, a shared understanding passing between them. Their love story had reached a new chapter, one that would see them through the highs and lows, the laughter and tears, and the countless memories they would create together.

The townspeople erupted in applause, their cheers ringing like a chorus of celebration. Amidst the wildflowers and the warm summer breeze, Lucas and Emma's union was not just a joining of two lives; it was a testament to the power of love, the strength of commitment, and the beauty of a journey that had led them to this moment in the heart of Hollow.

Their love story continued to unfold beyond the wedding day. In the months that followed, as the leaves began to change, and the town prepared for the colder months, Lucas and Emma received news that would shape the next chapter of their lives.

On that day, the morning sun cast a warm glow into the kitchen as Emma moved about, her movements purposeful and a smile tugging at the corners of her lips. The aroma of sizzling bacon and brewing coffee filled the air, a promise of a delicious breakfast in the making. Today was special, and she couldn't wait to share her news with Lucas.

As the final touches were added to the plates, Emma set a beautifully arranged breakfast on the table. Fluffy pancakes, a side of crispy bacon, and a colorful fruit salad created a feast that was both visually appealing and mouthwatering.

Lucas entered the kitchen, his steps slowing as he took in the spread before him. "Wow, Emma, this looks amazing," he said with genuine appreciation.

She beamed at him, her heart fluttering with a mix of excitement and nervousness. "I thought we could have a special breakfast today."

Lucas chuckled, pulling out a chair and taking a seat. "Well, it's definitely a wonderful way to start the day."

As they began to eat, Emma watched him closely, waiting for the perfect moment to reveal her news. She picked up a piece of bacon, her fingers wrapping around it as she spoke, a playful glint in her eyes. "You know, I've been thinking a lot about the ingredients that make up our lives."

Lucas raised an eyebrow, his interest piqued. "Ingredients?"

Emma nodded, her smile growing. "Yeah. Each ingredient brings its own flavor and uniqueness to the mix, just like we do in our relationship."

Lucas chuckled, taking a sip of his coffee. "You're always full of thoughtful metaphors, Emma."

She giggled softly. "Well, this one is particularly important." She picked up a strawberry from the fruit salad, holding it up for him to see. "For instance, this strawberry represents something sweet and delightful."

Lucas's curiosity deepened, and he leaned in a bit. "Okay, I'm listening."

Emma's heart raced as she continued, her voice a mix of playfulness and sincerity. "And this piece of bacon..." She paused for dramatic effect, then held it up, her eyes locked onto his. "This represents something a bit unexpected, with its own unique flavor."

Recognition slowly dawned on Lucas's face, and his eyes widened with realization. "Emma, are you..."

She nodded, her smile now beaming with joy. "I am. Lucas, we're having a baby."

His expression transformed from surprise to pure elation, his eyes sparkling with happiness. "You're serious?"

Emma's laughter filled the room as she nodded again. "Yes, yes, I am."

Lucas jumped up from his chair, his excitement barely contained as he crossed the short distance between them. He knelt down beside her, his hands cupping her face as he planted a heartfelt kiss on her lips. "Emma, that's incredible news!"

As they pulled away, his eyes held hers, his voice a mixture of joy and gratitude. "You've given me another amazing ingredient to our lives, something to cherish and celebrate."

Emma's heart swelled with his response, her own happiness mirrored in his eyes. "I'm so glad you're happy, Lucas."

He chuckled softly, his fingers brushing against her cheek. "Happy doesn't even begin to describe it."

They shared a tender moment, the warmth of their connection enhanced by the joy of the news they now shared. And as they returned to their breakfast, every bite seemed to carry an extra dose of sweetness, an ingredient that spoke of a future filled with love, laughter, and the beautiful journey of parenthood ahead.

With the support of their newfound family in Hollow, Lucas and Emma embarked on the journey of parenthood, embracing the challenges and joys that came with it. And when the time came, amidst the vibrant colors of autumn, their baby boy entered the world, a testament to the love that had grown and flourished in the embrace of a small town that had become their home.

As Lucas held their son for the first time, surrounded by the same gravestones that had once stood as silent witnesses, he couldn't help but feel a profound sense of gratitude. Their journey—from whispers among gravestones to the celebration of life and love—had been nothing short of extraordinary, a testament to the enduring power of connection, commitment, and the beauty of finding love in unexpected places.

CHAPTER EIGHT

Shadows of Unspoken Truth

The years passed like a gentle breeze, carrying with them the laughter of a young boy named Colt. He had inherited his father's quiet strength and his mother's vibrant spirit, a combination that endeared him to everyone in Hollow. The town had become his playground, and the people were his extended family

One day, Lucas walked alongside Colt as they strolled through the picturesque streets of Hollow. The sun was shining, casting a warm glow over the charming town, and the gentle breeze carried with it a sense of contentment. Colt's excitement was palpable, and his blue eyes sparkled with curiosity and energy.

As they walked, Colt's gaze was constantly scanning their surroundings, and his attention was quickly captured by a vibrant red ball that lay abandoned on the sidewalk. With a delighted shout, he picked it up and bounced it in his hands.

"Dad, look! A ball!" Colt exclaimed, his enthusiasm infectious.

Lucas smiled, his eyes crinkling at the corners. "Looks like you found a treasure, Colt."

Colt's grin widened as he held the ball in one hand, his energy spilling over.

"Watch this, Dad!" Without hesitation, he bounced the ball towards Ms. Hutchinson, a nearby shopkeeper, his voice ringing out with a cheerful greeting. "Hey, catch!"

Ms. Hutchinson, a friendly middle-aged woman, caught the ball with a surprised laugh. "Well, hello there! Thanks for the toss!"

Colt's charm was undeniable as he interacted with Ms. Hutchinson, his confidence shining through. "You're welcome! My name's Colt, and this is my dad, Lucas."

Lucas nodded with a friendly smile, pleased to see his son engaging so openly with others. "Nice to meet you."

Colt's interactions continued as they walked further, each exchange marked by his outgoing nature. He passed the ball to a group of children playing in a park, shared a laugh with a baker as he bounced it back, and even engaged in a brief game of catch with a friendly dog and its owner.

As they strolled, Lucas couldn't help but admire Colt's ability to make connections with people so effortlessly. His son's enthusiasm was like a magnet, drawing smiles and camaraderie wherever they went.

"Dad, this is fun!" Colt exclaimed, his eyes alight with happiness as he caught the ball once again.

Lucas chuckled, a sense of pride welling up within him. "You're right, Colt. It is."

They continued their walk, each bounce of the ball a small adventure that brought them closer to the heart of the town and the people who inhabited it. Colt's outgoing and charming nature was like a ray of sunshine, brightening the day for everyone they encountered.

As they rounded a corner and headed back towards the town square, Colt passed the ball to an elderly couple sitting on a bench. "Here you go! Have some fun!"

The couple exchanged a surprised glance before bursting into laughter, their joy infectious. "Well, aren't you a charmer!" the woman exclaimed, patting the empty spot on the bench next to her. "Come, sit for a moment."

Colt grinned and glanced at his dad, excitement still shining in his eyes. "Dad, can we?"

Lucas nodded, his heart swelling with warmth as he joined them on the bench. As they shared a few stories and laughs with the couple, Lucas realized that the ball Colt had found wasn't just a toy—it was a bridge that connected them to the people and the heart of the town they both cherished.

In that simple walk through town, Lucas saw his son's ability to bring happiness to others, to connect and engage with people from all walks of life. And as they continued their stroll, Lucas knew that with Colt by his side, every moment was a chance to make a new friend and create lasting memories.

Amidst Colt's joyous laughter, a shadow began to creep into Lucas's life. He began to feel weak, so he went to the local doctor's office. He did not want to tell Emma, so he went without her knowledge.

On that day, the sterile scent of the doctor's office surrounded Lucas as he sat on the examination table, his heart pounding in his chest. Doctor Jones, with a serious expression on his face, delivered the news that would change his life forever.

"Lucas," Doctor Jones began gently, "I'm afraid the test results confirm our suspicions. You have a rare and relentless disease."

Lucas's breath caught, his eyes widening with a mix of shock and disbelief. He cleared his throat, his voice betraying a tremor. "What kind of disease?"

The doctor's gaze held empathy as they continued. "You have Sarcoma, it is a type of cancerous tumor that develops in bone and/or soft tissue. Lucas. I'm sorry but you have stage IV Sarcoma, and it has spread all throughout your body and tissues."

The weight of the words settled heavily on Lucas's shoulders, and he struggled to comprehend the gravity of the situation. "What does this mean for me?"

The doctor's tone remained gentle yet honest. 'I won't sugarcoat it, Lucas. Stage IV Sarcoma is rare and particularly challenging. This is why you have felt swelling in so many areas of your body"

Lucas's mind raced as he processed the information. "What about treatment? Is there a cure?"

The doctor's expression grew somber. "I wish I could say yes. Unfortunately, with stage IV it makes itself uncurable. We can manage the symptoms and work to slow down the progression, but it's a battle that would require a miracle from above."

A mixture of fear and determination filled Lucas's eyes. "So, what do I do now?"

The doctor's gaze softened, conveying understanding. "We'll focus on maintaining your quality of life, managing the symptoms, and supporting you every step of the way. But you should know, the survival rate is extremely low."

Lucas stood at a crossroads, the weight of his diagnosis heavy on his shoulders. Despite the gravity of his rare disease, he found himself grappling with the decision to keep it hidden from his family. The thought of burdening them with his struggles and worrying their hearts weighed heavily on his mind. He believed that shielding them from the harsh reality of his condition was an act of love, a way to spare them pain. With a heavy sigh, he resolved to face his battle alone, believing that his strength would be enough to carry him through the challenges that lay ahead.

Lucas's love for Emma and Colt was immeasurable, and he found himself torn between his desire to protect them and his yearning for more time with them. He spent quiet nights researching, seeking a way to prolong his time with his family. He feared the pain of seeing the worry etched onto Emma's face and the confusion in Colt's eyes.

Weeks turned into months, and Lucas's condition deteriorated. His visits to the cemetery, once filled with purpose and dedication, became moments of quiet reflection. He watched as Colt ran among the gravestones, his laughter echoing through the air, and his heart ached at the thought of leaving him behind.

CHAPTER NINE

Unveiling Truths Too Late

E mma's intuition had always been keen, and as the months passed, she couldn't ignore the subtle changes in Lucas. His once-vibrant eyes held a weariness that she hadn't noticed before, and his steps were no longer as steady as they had been.

One afternoon, under the gentle sunlight, Lucas, Emma, and Colt strolled through the serene cemetery. The air was filled with a sense of quiet reflection, interrupted only by Colt's occasional laughter as he skipped around the gravestones. He tagged Lucas, and the two of them started a playful chase, their footsteps echoing among the memorials.

"Tag, you're it!" Colt's voice rang out with infectious enthusiasm.

Lucas joined in the game, a smile lighting up his face as he pursued his son. Their laughter harmonized with the rustling leaves, creating a joyful melody. However, in the midst of their game, a sudden coughing fit seized Lucas, forcing him to pause and clutch his chest.

Emma's worry was immediate as she rushed to his side, her hand resting on his back. "Lucas, are you okay?"

Kneeling down beside him, Lucas nodded weakly between coughs. "Yeah, I'm fine."

Colt's concern was evident as he peered at his father, brows furrowed. "Dad, are you sure?"

Emma's gaze flickered from Colt to Lucas, concern deepening as she took in the worry lines etched on Lucas's face. "Lucas, that cough doesn't sound good. Have you been feeling okay?"

Lucas managed a reassuring smile, attempting to alleviate their concern. "It's probably just a minor cold or something. Don't worry."

Lucas's attempt to downplay his condition didn't go unnoticed by Emma. She knew that he was trying to protect them, but she also knew that ignoring his health wouldn't solve anything. As they continued their walk through the rows of gravestones, Emma's determination to ensure Lucas's well-being grew stronger, and she silently vowed to uncover the truth and offer him the same care and support he had always shown them.

She waited until after Colt had been tucked into bed to confront Lucas. He was on the couch, staring at the fireplace. She sat down next to him and urged him to share what was burdening his heart.

"Lucas," Emma's voice held a mixture of concern and affection, "there's something in your eyes, something you're carrying all by yourself. Please, let me share the burden."

Lucas hesitated, the weight of his diagnosis pressing on him, his love for his family warring with his desire to shield them from pain. Yet, as he looked into Emma's eyes and saw the genuine care she held for him, he felt a crack forming in the walls he had built around his secret.

"Okay," he said, giving in. With a sigh, he began to unravel the truth, the rare and relentless disease that had invaded his body, casting a shadow over his life.

Emma's heart clenched as his words hung in the air, the weight of the revelation settling heavily on both of them. She moved closer, her arms encircling him in a comforting embrace. Her own emotions swirled, a maelstrom of worry, anger, and a fierce determination.

"Lucas," she whispered, her voice filled with both sadness and resolve, "we're in this together. You don't have to carry this burden alone. We'll face it head-on, fight against the darkness that threatens to consume us. You're not alone in this battle."

But time was no longer on their side, and the reality of their situation cast a pall over their days.

As the seasons changed once more, Lucas's condition worsened, and the once-bustling home felt heavy with unspoken emotions. Colt's laughter, though still present, seemed to carry a weight he couldn't understand, a weight that Lucas bores heavily upon his shoulders.

The End Chapter: Resonance of Eternity

On a quiet morning, with the sun casting a gentle glow over the town, Lucas's final moments arrived.

Emma gripped Lucas's hand tightly, her tears mingling with the raindrops that fell around them. Her voice trembled as she whispered her love, her heart heavy with the weight of impending loss.

"I love you, Lucas. You've filled my life with light, and I'll carry your love with me forever."

Colt stood nearby, his young eyes filled with a mix of understanding and grief. He had witnessed the depth of his parents' love, a love that had shaped his world and provided a foundation for his own sense of security. The rain seemed to echo the emotions of the moment, a bittersweet backdrop to the final moments they shared.

As Lucas's breaths grew shallower, Emma's grip on his hand tightened, as if trying to anchor him to this world a little longer. Her tears flowed freely, but her voice remained strong, a testament to the strength she drew from their love. "You're not alone, Lucas. We're in this together, always."

And then, with a final exhale, Lucas's struggle came to an end.

The town of Hollow, which had been the witness to so many of their shared moments, seemed to hold its breath in mourning, as if the very essence of the town grieved the loss of one of its beloved residents.

But just as the silence settled like a heavy shroud, a new voice emerged from the stillness. It was Colt's voice, young yet steady, breaking through the sorrow with a message of hope. "Thank you, Dad, for everything. Your love will stay with us, always."

As Colt's words hung in the air, a ray of sunlight pierced through the clouds, casting a warm glow over the scene.

Emma sobbed, the overwhelming wave of sorrow washing over her.

Colt put his hand on her shoulder. Emma expected him to offer words of comfort, but instead, he surprised her.

"Mom," Colt began, his gaze steady and his voice filled with a wisdom beyond his years. "There's something I need to tell you."

Emma looked at her son, her heart heavy yet curious. She listened as Colt unveiled a truth that left her breathless, a truth that defied the boundaries of life and death, a truth that bound their family in a way she could never have imagined.

"Mom," Colt continued, his voice resolute, "I am not just your son; I am also Dad's twin brother. God sent me back to be born to my twin brother and now father, bridging the gap that life had unjustly denied us. Both of us deserved a chance to have a brotherly relationship, and that's why I'm here.

You see as God our father allowed this then, he also in his graceful way chose to reignite our destined souls once more."

Emma stared at her son, stunned. She furrowed her eyebrows as she processed the weight of his words.

"Mom," Colt whispered once more.

"Yes Colt", Emma said.

"This is why Dad had always paid particular attention to those two grave sites, the one on the left is where he will rest, and the one on the right is where my first soul lays."

"Oh, Colt," Emma whispers, "so you're saying..."

Colt interrupts "yes mom God chose you to be the bright and shining light that brightened the path to our reunion, thank you and I love you mom."

Emma's eyes widened, her heart catching in her throat as she looked into Colt's eyes, a familiar gaze, a gaze that held the essence of the man she had loved and lost. In that moment, the pieces fell into place, and the truth resonated deep within her soul.

As Colt's words lingered in the air, the wind seemed to carry them across the town, across the gravestones that had witnessed their journey. It was a story that defied time, which transcended the boundaries of the universe, a story of love that had come full circle.

And as Hollow embraced its newest chapter, one that held both loss and discovery, the legacy of Lucas's love lived on, woven into the tapestry of a family that had found each other across the edges of life and death, a family that had been bound by love, by destiny, and by a bond that could never be broken.